THE GIGANTIC BEAR

Level 5E

Written by Louise Goodman
Illustrated by Sarah Vonthron-Laver

What is synthetic phonics?

Synthetic phonics teaches children to recognise the sounds of letters and to blend (synthesise) them together to make whole words.

Understanding sound/letter relationships gives children the confidence and ability to read unfamiliar words, without having to rely on memory or guesswork; this helps them to progress towards independent reading.

Did you know? Spoken English uses more than 40 speech sounds. Each sound is called a *phoneme*. Some phonemes relate to a single letter (d-o-g) and others to combinations of letters (sh-ar-p). When a phoneme is written down it is called a *grapheme*. Teaching these sounds, matching them to their written form and sounding out words for reading is the basis of synthetic phonics.

Consultant

I love reading phonics has been created in consultation with language expert Abigail Steel. She has a background in teaching and teacher training and is a respected expert in the field of synthetic phonics. Abigail Steel is a regular contributor to educational publications. Her international education consultancy supports parents and teachers in the promotion of literacy skills.

Reading tips

 This book focuses on the j sound, made with the letters g, ge and dge, as in gent, gin, gym, barge and hedge.

Tricky words in this book

Any words in bold may have unusual spellings or are new and have not yet been introduced.

Tricky words in this book:

place everyone was busy their listen giraffes genies voice would you

Extra ways to have fun with this book

After the reader has read the story, ask them questions about what they have just read:

Who tried to make the bear go away?
Why did the bear go to the village?

A gigantic bear, come here? Stop telling tall tales!

A pronunciation guide

This grid contains the sounds used in the stories in levels 4, 5 and 6 and a guide on how to say them. /a/ represents the sounds made, rather than the letters in a word.

/ai/ as in game	/ai/ as in play/they	/ee/ as in leaf/these	/ee/ as in he
/igh/ as in kite/light	/igh/ as in find/sky	/oa/ as in home	/oa/ as in snow
/oa/ as in cold	/y+oo/ as in cube/music/new	long /oo/ as in flute/crew/blue	/oi/ as in boy
/er/ as in bird/hurt	/or/ as in snore/oar/door	/or/ as in dawn/sauce/walk	/e/ as in head
/e/ as in said/any	/ou/ as in cow	/u/ as in touch	/air/ as in hare/bear/there
/eer/ as in deer/here/cashier	/t/ as in tripped/skipped	/d/ as in rained	/j/ as in gent/gin/gym
/j/ as in barge/hedge	/s/ as in cent/circus/cyst	/s/ as in prince	/s/ as in house
/ch/ as in itch/catch	/w/ as in white	/h/ as in who	/r/ as in write/rhino

Sounds this story focuses on are highlighted in the grid.

/f/ as in phone	/f/ as in rough	/ul/ as in pencil/hospital	/z/ as in fries/cheese/breeze
/n/ as in knot/gnome/engine	/m/ as in welcome/thumb/column	/g/ as in guitar/ghost	/zh/ as in vision/beige
/k/ as in chord	/k/ as in plaque/bouquet	/nk/ as in uncle	/ks/ as in box/books/ducks/cakes
/a/ and /o/ as in hat/what	/e/ and /ee/ as in bed/he	/i/ and /igh/ as in fin/find	/o/ and /oa/ as in hot/cold
/u/ and short /oo/ as in but/put	/ee/, /e/ and /ai/ as in eat/bread/break	/igh/, /ee/ and /e/ as in tie/field/friend	/ou/ and /oa/ as in cow/blow
/ou/, /oa/ and /oo/ as in out/shoulder/could	/i/ and /ai/ as in money/they	/c/ and /s/ as in cat/cent	/y/, /igh/ and /i/ as in yes/sky/myth
/g/ and /j/ as in got/giant	/ch/, /c/ and /sh/ as in chin/school/chef	/er/, /air/ and /eer/ as in earth/bear/ears	/u/, /ou/ and /oa/ as in plough/dough

Be careful not to add an 'uh' sound to 's', 't', 'p', 'c', 'h', 'r', 'm', 'd', 'g', 'l', 'f' and 'b'. For example, say 'fff' not 'fuh' and 'sss' not 'suh'.

Once upon a time, there was a
place called Tale Town.
In the day **everyone was busy.**

Sailors fished on **their** barges,
farmers milked cows, bakers
baked and kids flew kites.

But when the moon rose in the sky, everyone gathered by the old oak tree, to **listen** to a

story from Grandma. Even when
it rained or snowed, they still
came – she was a genius.

She told them legends of giants and danger, **giraffes** and gems, gingerbread men and **genies** from Egypt.

But one night, a sailor ran
over the bridge, yelling:
"A bear, a bear! He's gigantic –
and he's here!"
"An emergency!" cried the chief
of the village. He was large.
"I'll handle this!"

But he couldn't.

"A challenge!" cried Gerald the
farmer. He was huge.
"I'll make that bear buzz off!"

But he couldn't.

"Charge!" cried Germaine the baker. She was agile and good at dodging.
"I'll put that bear in a cage."

But she couldn't.

"What shall we do!" cried the villagers.

Then a small **voice** said:
"I'll have a go." It was Grandma!

Grandma walked over to the
bear and said gently:
"Excuse me, Bear. **Would you**
like to hear a story?"

"Yes!" cried the bear.
"That's what I came here for!"

Everyone gathered by the
old oak tree – including the
bear – for Grandma's story.

It was her best yet.

OVER 48 TITLES IN SIX LEVELS

Abigail Steel recommends...

Some titles from Level 4

I love reading phonics — **The Circus Mice** — 978-1-84898-582-7

I love reading phonics — **Monster's Night** — 978-1-84898-583-4

I love reading phonics — **The Mummy Code** — 978-1-84898-585-8

Other titles to enjoy from Level 5

I love reading phonics — **Celebrity Celia** — 978-1-84898-587-2

I love reading phonics — **The Cemetery Dance** — 978-1-84898-588-9

I love reading phonics — **Goose Flight** — 978-1-84898-589-6

Some titles from Level 6

I love reading phonics — **Hugh is New** — 978-1-84898-590-2

I love reading phonics — **Clumsy Eagle** — 978-1-84898-591-9

I love reading phonics — **Bad Zombie Movie** — 978-1-84898-592-6

An Hachette UK Company
www.hachette.co.uk

Copyright © Octopus Publishing Group Ltd 2012
First published in Great Britain in 2012 by TickTock, an imprint of Octopus Publishing Group Ltd,
Endeavour House, 189 Shaftesbury Avenue, London WC2H 8JY.
www.octopusbooks.co.uk

ISBN 978 1 84898 586 5

Printed and bound in China
10 9 8 7 6 5 4 3 2 1